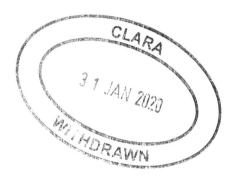

CLARA

3 1 JAN 2020

WITHDRAWN

Can YOU spot the Nasty
Splash hidden in the story?

For Oscar, a young artist who draws his own wicked pictures.

Oisín McGann was born in 1973 and he still hasn't grown up. Nobody knows why. He began writing and illustrating stories not long after he started school. That's fine for a kid, but ten years later he left school and went to college to learn drawing and painting ... and he was *still* writing silly children's stories. Oisín kept on making up kids' stories while he tried working in a bunch of different grown-up jobs. In the end, adult work was too serious for him. So now he makes children's books for a living.

His mother hopes he will grow up and get a proper job some time soon.

Oisín has made up more stuff about Lenny and his grandad in **Mad Grandad's Flying Saucer**, **Mad Grandad's Robot Garden** **Mad Grandad and the Mutant River** and **Mad Grandad and the Kleptoes**.

Mad Grandad's
WICKED PICTURES

Oisín McGann

THE O'BRIEN PRESS
DUBLIN

First published 2007 by The O'Brien Press Ltd,
12 Terenure Road East, Rathgar, Dublin 6, Ireland.
Tel: +353 1 4923333; Fax: +353 1 4922777
E-mail: books@obrien.ie
Website: www.obrien.ie
Reprinted 2009 (twice), 2010.

ISBN: 978-1-84717-063-7

Copyright for text & illustrations © Oisín McGann
Copyright for typesetting, layout, design
© The O'Brien Press Ltd.

All rights reserved. No part of this publication may be
reproduced or utilised in any form or by any means,
electronic or mechanical, including photocopying, recording
or in any information storage and retrieval system, without
permission in writing from the publisher.

British Library Cataloguing-in-Publication Data
McGann, Oisin
Mad Grandad's wicked pictures
1. Mad Grandad (Fictitious character) - Juvenile fiction
2. Lenny (Fictitious character) - Juvenile fiction
3. Grandfathers - Juvenile fiction 4. Children's stories
I. Title
823.9'2[J]

4 5 6 7 8 9 10
10 11 12 13

Class: JBR
Acc: 10/8968
Ref: 10/327
€ 5.99

The O'Brien Press receives assistance from

Layout and design: The O'Brien Press Ltd.
Illustrations: Oisín McGann
Printed in Germany by Bercker
The paper in this book is produced using pulp from
managed forests.

CHAPTER 1

Patterns in the Paint

It was the middle of the holidays, and I was going over to Grandad's house to help him paint his living-room.

When I got there, the room was already cleared out and there were sheets over the furniture. There was a bunch of old tins and tubes of **paint** sitting on the floor.

'Where did you get those, Grandad?' I asked.

'They've been in the shed for ages, Lenny,' Grandad said. 'I bought some of this paint in the **nineteen-sixties**!'

The nineteen-sixties was years ago, and Grandad talked about that time a lot. I think it's because he wasn't **bald** back then.

Grandad was a bit **mad**. He sometimes put orange juice in his tea, or **danced** when he was listening to the news on the radio.

'Does paint that old still work?'
I asked Grandad.

'Only one way to find out!'
Grandad replied.

He opened one of the tins. The
paint was a pale yellow. Dipping
a brush in it, he reached up and
painted a piece of the wall. That
was when things went **weird**.

The paint was **striped**. The stripes were red and yellow.

'Holy smoke!' Grandad gasped.

He brushed on more of the striped paint and we looked at it in amazement. He tried another tin. This paint was green with yellow **polka dots**. He just brushed it onto the wall and the dots appeared all neat and clear.

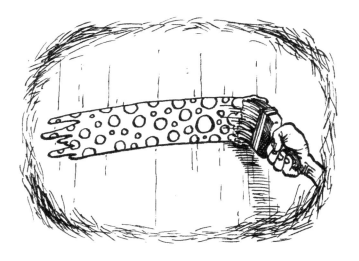

'Let's see what else we've got!' I said.

CHAPTER 2

Named and Framed

We opened more tins and started painting. I did a separate patch of wall. All of the tins of paint had **weird** patterns in them.

A few minutes later, we stood back to look at our work.

'That's **mad**,' I said.

15

'I have dreams about things like this,' Grandad told me. 'They almost look like **creatures**, don't they?'

Grandad's creature was much bigger than mine, but mine had sharper teeth.

'Yeah! This is cool!' I said. 'Pity we have to paint over them.'

'Who says we have to?' Grandad replied.

'Great! I'm going to call my one **Fang**,' I told him.

'I think I'll call my one **Mildred**,' Grandad said, nodding to himself.

He disappeared out the door and came back a minute later with a picture frame.

'I've had this lying about for ages,' he said.

He hammered a picture hook
in over my painting and hung
the frame on it. It made my
picture look really **cool**.

'Now we just have to get a **frame** for mine and they'll both look like **proper** paintings!' he told me.

That sounded like a great idea. Grandad took some **measurements** for his picture and then we headed into town to get a frame.

CHAPTER 3

The Missing Picture

When we came back from the
framing shop, I hurried into the
living-room. I skidded to a stop
and **stared** at the wall.

'Grandad!' I called. 'My painting's **gone**!'

'Holy smoke!' he gasped as he came in. 'How did that happen?'

There was nothing but a **blank space** on the wall where Fang had been. Even the frame was gone. We both went over and touched the wall just to be sure.

'Look!' Grandad said, pointing at the **floor**.

There were little drops of paint on the floor, leading out the door.

'Somebody **stole** it!' Grandad growled.

'But it was painted on the wall,' I said. 'How can you steal paint from a wall?'

We followed the **trail** of paint drops out into the hall. We followed it up the stairs. Then we followed it into Grandad's spare room.

As we walked in, a **movement** above us made us look up. The picture frame suddenly dropped from the ceiling and fell over us. It landed on the floor with a thump.

I went to step out of it, but found I could only **slide** along the floor instead. I was completely **flat** and I was stuck to the floor!

'Grandad, what's going on?' I yelled.

Grandad was **stuck** too.

'It's like we've been turned into
paintings, Lenny!' Grandad told me.
'But I can still move.'

'Me too,' I said.

We heard a nasty laugh from above us. Sitting on top of the door was my painting, **Fang**. He was real and round and he looked like a crazy little **goblin**.

He jumped down, picked up the
picture frame and ran downstairs.

CHAPTER 4

Driven up the Walls

'After him!' Grandad shouted. 'If he used that frame to make us like this, maybe we can use it to get back to **normal**!'

But that was going to be harder than it sounded. We could run across the floor, or over the walls and along the ceiling – we could even go round corners. But we were still completely **flat**.

We rushed along the walls, down over the stairs. Then we crept over the hall ceiling towards the living-room.

Fang was inside, whispering something to Grandad's painting, **Mildred**.

Mildred was a mad mix of **spiky** legs, loads of eyes and a striped body. She was moving now too. But she must have been too big to fit through the frame because she was still flat on the wall. She **sniggered** to herself when Fang made some joke. Then she saw us.

With a **roar**, she came
charging after us.

'Run, Lenny!' Grandad yelped.

When Mildred opened her mouth, she was all eyes and teeth and claws. We knew right then that she would **eat** us if she caught us.

So we ran. We dodged round plug sockets, down walls, up corners, around light switches, and through the crack of the closed door into the kitchen.

Mildred chased us across the kitchen cupboards and over the counter. We **slipped** and **skidded** around the sink, over the draining board and down to the floor again.

The tiles were slippery too – it was like trying to crawl over **ice**. Mildred couldn't keep her grip and she kept flying past us as we turned to avoid her.

We scooted up the wall and across the window. We were so thin, the light shone through us like an **X-ray**.

Fang appeared out of nowhere. He jumped onto the counter and grabbed the **kettle**.

'Look out, Lenny!' Grandad shouted. 'That water could **wipe** us out!'

Fang threw the water up onto the window and it splashed above us. Some of it got on my trousers and nearly washed away my **bum**!

Grandad lost a bit more hair when the water swept past his head – but he was mostly **bald** anyway.

Mildred ducked under the dripping water, still chasing us. Grandad suddenly had an idea. He turned and **spat** at the monster. She skidded to a stop as the spit hit her. But it wasn't water, it was just **paint** like the rest of us.

That only made her madder. She charged after Grandad ... and then realized that she'd stopped for too long. The drips of water came down around her like **bars**, cutting her off.

'That won't hold her for long,' Grandad said. 'Let's go!'

CHAPTER 5

Terror in the Cellar

Fang wiped the glass dry with some
kitchen roll before Mildred could be
washed away. Then he threw more
water at us as we raced across the
floor-tiles.

The water **blocked** the kitchen
door, so we had to turn and run
another way. Fang giggled.
Mildred came after us again.

There was a wet mop in the corner and we ducked behind it. Mildred was running so fast she nearly ran into it. She turned at the last second, but her feet rubbed against the mop.

Howling, she dragged smears of wet paint across the floor.

We made it to the cellar door
and slipped underneath.

'There's no way out of here,
Lenny,' Grandad said. 'If we don't
find a way to stop her, we're
going to get **gobbled** up.'

The cellar was full of all sorts of
stuff. It was dark too, and when
Mildred came under the door after us
she couldn't see where we were. There
was a big **circus poster** on the wall
and we hid underneath it.

'Lenny, look!' Grandad
muttered, pointing at something.

There, behind some boxes, was
another **picture frame**.

'Maybe we can use that,' he
said.

But Mildred must have heard him.
She suddenly turned and came **racing**
towards us.

Grandad pushed me towards the picture frame. Then he slid out from behind the poster, waving his arms and shouting. Mildred snarled, charging at him with her **mouth** open.

CHAPTER 6

Paper, Paint and Panic

I darted down to the picture frame. As soon as I ducked behind it, I could feel something **pull** me from the wall and I fell out of the frame. I was back to **normal**. I wasn't flat any more.

Pushing the boxes out of the way, I jumped up and looked over at Grandad.

Mildred came flying at him. He scampered back under the poster and out the other side. Mildred was only **inches** behind him.

I didn't know what else to do, so I **slapped** my hands against the poster. Mildred stopped suddenly. She was stuck fast to the poster. I rubbed my hand over the rest of it and I could feel her **sticking** to the back of the paper.

'Pull it off the wall, Lenny!'
Grandad yelled.

I grabbed the poster and tore it
off the wall. Mildred came with it,
caught on the back of the sheet of
paper.

Grandad hurried down to the
picture frame and hopped through,
landing on top of the boxes with a
crash.

'Right,' he said as he looked at Mildred on the back of the poster. 'I wonder if the other one sticks to paper too?'

Mildred gave a whimper and thrashed around a bit, but she was totally **trapped**.

Fang was in the living-room, trying to get the tops off the tins of paint. He wanted to create **more** paint creatures. But the lids were old and jammed up with paint and were hard to open.

He was about to prise one open with a screwdriver when I leaned round the doorway and shouted at him:

'Hey! Come and get me you horrible little ... **paint-thing**!'

Fang looked up at me in **surprise**. Then he hissed and bared his teeth. His claws scratched over the floor as he came running after me.

But Grandad was ready for him. Fang ran into the hall ... and right onto some wallpaper that Grandad was unrolling along the floor. The paint creature's feet **stuck** to the paper and he skidded into the wall with the paper curling up around him.

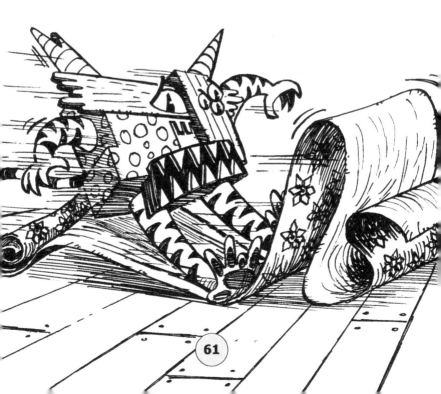

As Fang tried to get free, Grandad charged up and dropped the **picture frame** over the creature. Then he quickly picked it up again.

Fang found himself trapped as a **painting** again. But this time, he was painted onto wallpaper. We thought he deserved it. We rolled up the big poster and the piece of wallpaper and put them in the **recycling** bin.

With a bit of luck, they'll end up being made into **toilet roll** or something useful like that.